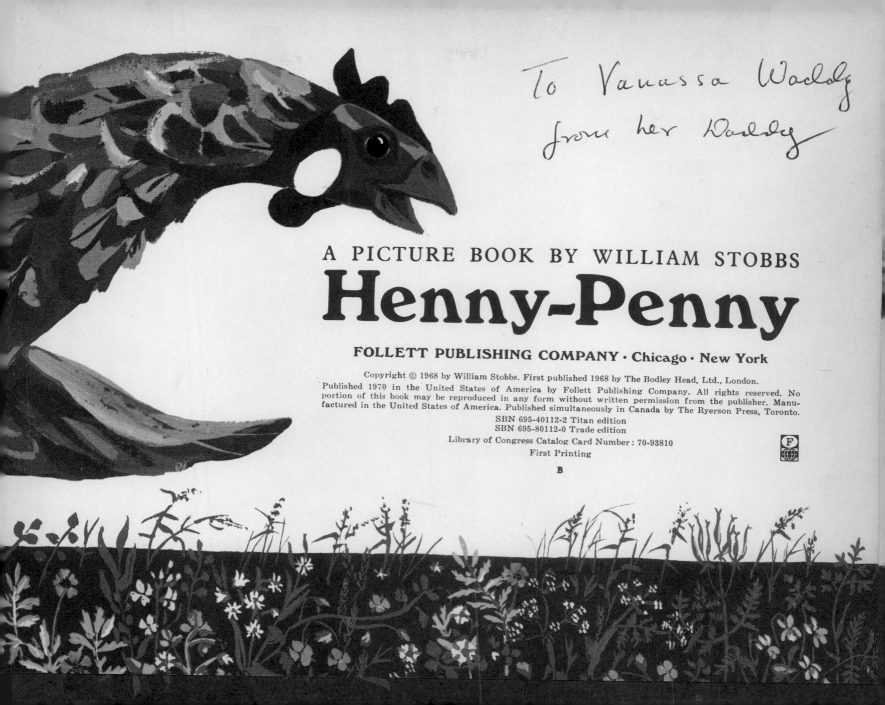

To Vanassa Waddly
from her Daddy

A PICTURE BOOK BY WILLIAM STOBBS

Henny-Penny

FOLLETT PUBLISHING COMPANY · Chicago · New York

Copyright © 1968 by William Stobbs. First published 1968 by The Bodley Head, Ltd., London.
Published 1970 in the United States of America by Follett Publishing Company. All rights reserved. No
portion of this book may be reproduced in any form without written permission from the publisher. Manu-
factured in the United States of America. Published simultaneously in Canada by The Ryerson Press, Toronto.

SBN 695-40112-2 Titan edition
SBN 695-80112-0 Trade edition
Library of Congress Catalog Card Number: 70-93810
First Printing

B

They went along and they went along, and they went along, till they met Ducky-daddles.

"Where are you going to, Henny-penny and Cocky-locky?" said Ducky-daddles.

"Oh! We're going to tell the king the sky's a-falling," said Henny-penny and Cocky-locky.

"May I come with you?" said Ducky-daddles.

"Certainly," said Henny-penny and Cocky-locky.

So Henny-penny, Cocky-locky, and
Ducky-daddles went to tell the king the
sky was a-falling.

So they went along, and they went along, and they went along, till they met Goosey-poosey. "Where are you going to, Henny-penny, Cocky-locky, and Ducky-daddles?" said Goosey-poosey.

"Oh! We're going to tell the king the sky's a-falling," said Henny-penny and Cocky-locky, and Ducky-daddles.

"May I come with you?" said Goosey-poosey.

"Certainly," said Henny-penny, Cocky-locky, and Ducky-daddles. So Henny-penny, Cocky-locky, Ducky-daddles, and Goosey-poosey went to tell the king the sky was a-falling.

So they went along, and they went along, and they went along, till they met Turkey-lurkey. "Where are you going, Henny-penny, Cocky-locky, Ducky-daddles, and Goosey-poosey?" said Turkey-lurkey.

"Oh! We're going to tell the king the sky's a-falling," said Henny-penny, Cocky-locky, Ducky-daddles, and Goosey-poosey.

"May I come with you, Henny-penny, Cocky-locky, Ducky-daddles, and Goosey-poosey?" said Turkey-lurkey.

"Oh, certainly, Turkey-lurkey," said Henny-penny, Cocky-locky, Ducky-daddles, and Goosey-poosey. So Henny-penny, Cocky-locky, Ducky-daddles, Goosey-poosey, and Turkey-lurkey all went to tell the king the sky was a-falling.

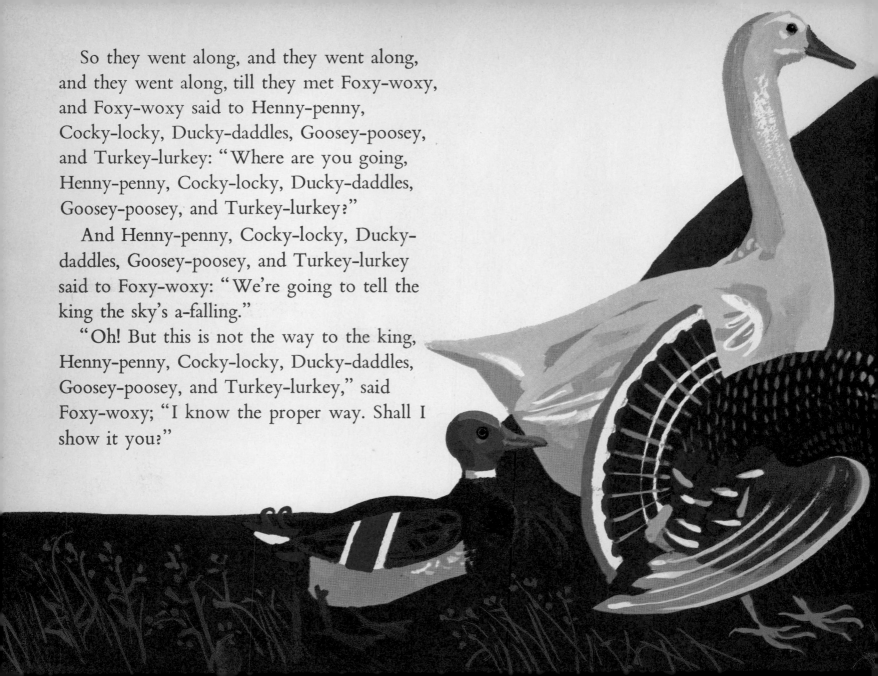

So they went along, and they went along,
and they went along, till they met Foxy-woxy,
and Foxy-woxy said to Henny-penny,
Cocky-locky, Ducky-daddles, Goosey-poosey,
and Turkey-lurkey: "Where are you going,
Henny-penny, Cocky-locky, Ducky-daddles,
Goosey-poosey, and Turkey-lurkey?"

And Henny-penny, Cocky-locky, Ducky-
daddles, Goosey-poosey, and Turkey-lurkey
said to Foxy-woxy: "We're going to tell the
king the sky's a-falling."

"Oh! But this is not the way to the king,
Henny-penny, Cocky-locky, Ducky-daddles,
Goosey-poosey, and Turkey-lurkey," said
Foxy-woxy; "I know the proper way. Shall I
show it you?"

"Oh, certainly, Foxy-woxy," said Henny-penny, Cocky-locky, Ducky-daddles, Goosey-poosey, and Turkey-lurkey. So Henny-penny, Cocky-locky, Ducky-daddles, Goosey-poosey, Turkey-lurkey, and Foxy-woxy all went to tell the king the sky was a-falling.

So they went along, and they went along, and they went along, till they came to a narrow and dark hole. Now this was the door of Foxy-woxy's cave. But Foxy-woxy said to Henny-penny, Cocky-locky, Ducky-daddles, Goosey-poosey, and Turkey-lurkey: "This is the short way to the king's palace: you'll soon get there if you follow me. I will go first and you come after, Henny-penny, Cocky-locky, Ducky-daddles, Goosey-poosey, and Turkey-lurkey."

"Why, of course, certainly, without doubt, why not?" said Henny-penny, Cocky-locky, Ducky-daddles, Goosey-poosey, and Turkey-lurkey.

So Foxy-woxy went into his cave, and he didn't go very far, but turned round to wait for Henny-penny, Cocky-locky, Ducky-daddles, Goosey-poosey, and Turkey-lurkey.

So first Turkey-lurkey went through the dark hole into the cave. He hadn't gone far when "Hrumph," Foxy-woxy snapped off Turkey-lurkey's head and threw his body over his left shoulder.

Then Goosey-poosey went in, and "Hrumph," off went her head and Goosey-poosey was thrown beside Turkey-lurkey.

Then Ducky-daddles waddled down, and "Hrumph" snapped Foxy-woxy, and Ducky-daddles' head was off and Ducky-daddles was thrown alongside Turkey-lurkey and Goosey-poosey.

Then Cocky-locky strutted down into the cave, and he hadn't gone far when "Snap, Hrumph!" went Foxy-woxy, and Cocky-locky was thrown alongside of Turkey-lurkey, Goosey-poosey, and Ducky-daddles.

But Foxy-woxy had made two bites at Cocky-locky, and when the first snap only hurt Cocky-locky, but didn't kill him, he called out to Henny-penny. But she turned tail and off she ran home, so she never told the king the sky was a-falling.